AF228567

# Law Enforcement

# SWAT

**Abdo & Daughters**
An imprint of Abdo Publishing | abdobooks.com

# John Hamilton

**ABDOBOOKS.COM**

Published by Abdo Publishing, a division of ABDO, PO Box 398166, Minneapolis, Minnesota 55439. Copyright © 2022 by Abdo Consulting Group, Inc. International copyrights reserved in all countries. No part of this book may be reproduced in any form without written permission from the publisher. Abdo & Daughters™ is a trademark and logo of Abdo Publishing.

Printed in the United States of America, North Mankato, Minnesota.
102021
012022

Editor: Sue Hamilton
Copy Editor: Bridget O'Brien
Creative Director: Dorothy Toth
Graphic Design: Sue Hamilton
Cover Design: Victoria Bates
Cover Photo: iStock
Interior Images: Alamy-pgs 5, 6, 10 & 43; AP-pgs 8, 9, 11, 12, 13, 14, 15, 16, 19, 21, 22, 23, 27, 35 & 36; Armor Express/Fearless-pg 30; Colt's Manufacturing Company-pg 33; Dallas Police Dept-pg 7; Defense Technology-pg 34 (bottom left); DVIDS-pg 32 (top right); GD-OTS Canada-pg 25; iStock-pgs 1, 28, 31 & 32 (top left); Kelsey Samuels-pg 26; Lenco Armored Vehicles-pg 37; Matthews Specialty Vehicles-pg 38; Rippel Effect-pg 34 (bottom right); Shutterstock-pgs 24, 29, 39, 41 & 45; SIG Sauer-pg 32 (bottom).

**LIBRARY OF CONGRESS CONTROL NUMBER: 2019956149**

**PUBLISHER'S CATALOGING-IN-PUBLICATION DATA**

Names: Hamilton, John, author.

Title: SWAT / by John Hamilton

Description: Minneapolis, Minnesota : Abdo Publishing, 2022 | Series: Law enforcement | Includes online resources and index

Identifiers: ISBN 9781532193880 (lib. bdg.) | ISBN 9781098212667 (ebook)

Subjects: LCSH: Law enforcement--Juvenile literature. | Police--Special weapons and tactics units--Juvenile literature. | Police forces--Juvenile literature.

Classification: DDC 363.2--dc23

# TABLE OF CONTENTS

# EXTREME THREATS

**A police officer is sent to a bank where a robbery is in** progress. When she arrives at the scene, a man with an assault rifle has barricaded himself inside. He threatens to kill hostages unless his demands are met.

Across town, an undercover police officer buys narcotics from a group of people living in a well-known drug house. He notices that the doors and windows are reinforced with steel bars and cages. The criminals inside are heavily armed. They will become violent if police try to arrest them.

Both of these situations require extra firepower and special tactics. When the regular police need help, they call in SWAT teams.

SWAT stands for Special Weapons and Tactics. SWAT teams are groups of specially trained law enforcement officers. They are well equipped, armed to the teeth, and ready to handle the most extreme crime scenes.

SWAT team members bring extra firepower to make arrests in dangerous situations.

SWAT officers marching in a parade. Their extreme training keeps people safe in the most dangerous situations.

SWAT team members are often called operators. They form elite units within most American police departments today. Only the most physically and mentally fit men and women are chosen. For example, the Dallas Police Department in Texas employs about 3,400 officers. Just a few dozen are members of the city's full-time SWAT unit.

SWAT operators have a passion for their work. It's a job most cops aren't suited for, but it is very rewarding. It's a chance to make a big difference in creating safer communities.

Only the most skilled officers become members of SWAT units.

# SWAT HISTORY

**In the 1960s, many Americans were worried about crime.** Political assassinations and violent protests against the Vietnam War rocked the country. Deadly riots broke out in many cities, spawned by poverty and racial unrest.

On August 1, 1966, a sniper climbed the clock tower at the University of Texas in Austin. He randomly shot and killed 14 people and wounded 31 others before he was finally killed by police.

In 1967, California's Los Angeles Police Department became the first to train rapid-response officers for violent, high-risk situations. The new SWAT division used military-type tactics and weapons for crime scenes that were too dangerous for regular patrol officers.

The University of Texas clock tower where a sniper took aim in 1966.

Other police departments soon formed their own SWAT teams. Today, almost all large cities include a SWAT unit. Some are called by different names, such as New York City's Emergency Service Unit, or the Special Threat Response Team of Miami, Florida. No matter what they are called, they all have the same mission: to handle high-risk situations using the best tactics and weapons available.

Members of the Yuba County, California, SWAT team at an active shooter drill.

SWAT teams have become a critical part of modern law enforcement. About 90 percent of cities with a population over 50,000 have SWAT teams. About 70 percent of smaller cities have them. That adds up to about 1,200 SWAT divisions nationwide.

Most SWAT teams are part-time units. Only large police forces can afford to employ full-time SWAT teams. Full-time units are on call 24 hours a day, 7 days a week. Cities with full-time SWAT departments include Los Angeles, California; Dallas, Texas; Atlanta, Georgia; Phoenix, Arizona; and Miami, Florida.

For smaller departments, SWAT operators also work as regular police officers. Most of their time is spent performing normal patrol cop duties. However, they are always on call for SWAT emergencies. Operators train together at least once a month on marksmanship skills, rescue operations, and physical fitness. They keep their SWAT equipment and weapons with them, often in the trunks of their patrol cars. When an emergency arises, they can arrive at a crime scene quickly, ready for action.

SWAT officers training with patrol cops.

# THE ROLE OF SWAT

**S**WAT operators use military-grade weapons and equipment. Their training prepares them to handle high-risk crime scenes without letting their guards down or leaving anything to chance. They are ready for almost any situation.

It is too dangerous to assume how suspects might behave at a crime scene. Some of the toughest-looking criminals give up easily when faced with a heavily armed SWAT team. On the other hand, mild-mannered people might snap at any moment and begin shooting. SWAT operators plan for all possibilities. Their forceful tactics are meant to confuse and intimidate criminals into giving up right away. The goal of SWAT is to have a peaceful ending for everybody, including the suspects.

A gang member is arrested by a heavily armed SWAT team.

Members of a Texas SWAT team prepare to advance on a house where a person is being held hostage.

There are many situations where police officers need special weapons and tactics. SWAT teams can be used during riots, undercover narcotics arrests ("buy-bust" operations), or terrorist attacks. They can even be called to protect high-risk people, such as presidents or governors, when they need to be transported through cities. The two most common assignments include barricade situations and serving high-risk warrants.

A man is taken into custody after barricading himself inside an apartment building.

## Barricade situations

When challenged by regular patrol cops, hostile criminals sometimes retreat to a house or other building. They barricade themselves inside. They might also take hostages. This makes the crime scene even more dangerous.

Barricade situations are also called armed standoffs. In law enforcement, they are called barricaded person operations, or BP calls. Regular patrol cops are usually the first ones on the scene. In these intense situations, the first responders are trained to call in a SWAT team instead of shooting it out with the suspects. A police commander issues a "full SWAT callout," which activates the unit. SWAT operators have the firepower and experience needed when a highly dangerous situation rapidly spirals out of control.

## High-risk warrants

The other most common role for SWAT teams is to serve warrants on violent criminals. Warrants are legal documents issued by judges. They allow law enforcement to make arrests or to search property.

Warrants are often issued for drug dealers who sell narcotics out of their houses, usually after an undercover investigation. Most of these "drug houses" are located in high-crime areas.

Oklahoma officers serve a search warrant at the home of a drive-by shooting suspect.

Many drug dealers possess firearms, which they use to protect themselves against rival dealers or gang members. The guns can also be used against police officers. When faced with such situations, SWAT teams are called to handle the arrests.

## ACTIVE SHOOTERS

School and workplace shootings have become a tragic part of modern life. An active shooter is a person with a gun who goes on a rampage and kills people seemingly at random. Most active shooting situations are finished by the time a SWAT team can arrive. That is why many patrol cops today carry high-powered rifles in their squad cars. Cops are trained to face these deadly situations immediately, without SWAT backup.

# Chapter 4

# JOINING SWAT

**E**xperienced police officers usually volunteer to join SWAT. Being accepted is an honor, and a chance to be part of an elite squad. With the right personality, it is a job that is both exciting and rewarding.

Police departments around the country have different requirements for joining SWAT. Most departments require at least two years of patrol duty before an officer is eligible. Past military experience helps, but it is not required.

## SWAT tryouts

After volunteering, candidates attend SWAT tryouts. Only the very best officers are chosen. It's not unusual to have 50 applicants for just two or three openings.

Tryouts include physical fitness tests. These usually include a vertical jump, bench press, push-ups, sit-ups, and a 1.5-mile (2.4 km) run. Candidates may also be required to finish a timed obstacle course in heavy SWAT gear.

Recruits who pass the physical fitness requirements must next show mastery of the firearms used by their departments. That includes short-barreled assault rifles (usually AR-15 or M4 carbines), shotguns, submachine guns, and sidearms.

In some big-city SWAT units, such as the department run in Miami, Florida, candidates move on to SWAT school. After several weeks of advanced training, candidates must pass a written exam. Finally, after graduation, they become a rookie SWAT team member.

Oklahoma FBI SWAT teams secure an apartment building during a training exercise.

# SWAT TRAINING

**I**t is a source of pride to be a SWAT operator. Team members train to stay in shape and keep their police skills as sharp as possible. They have to be mentally and physically strong, and they must be good team players. Most SWAT operators are men, but many women also have the physical and mental toughness required for the job.

## Training and trust

SWAT training can be grueling. Operators must maintain top physical conditioning and be ready for action at all times. The job requires quick thinking. However, operators are trained not to rush into dangerous situations. Reckless actions can get themselves or teammates killed. SWAT operators learn to follow orders and let their training guide their actions. They trust their teammates, and protect each other at all times.

Texas SWAT officers rehearse a vehicle takedown.

## Physical fitness

A typical day on a SWAT team often starts with physical fitness training. Operators stay in shape by lifting weights and long-distance running. Keeping fit is important so they can carry heavy equipment and weapons. They must also be agile and fast. They learn hand-to-hand fighting techniques to defend themselves and subdue violent suspects.

In addition to helping operators stay physically fit, regular workouts are also good for relieving stress. That is very important because SWAT work is filled with many life-or-death decisions, which can be hard to deal with mentally.

A SWAT officer crawls through sand on an obstacle course competition in Louisiana.

A SWAT officer participates in an accuracy competition in Virginia.

## Firearms training

SWAT operators learn which firearms—rifles, shotguns, sidearms, or submachine guns—are best for various situations. They spend hundreds of hours on police firing ranges. They shoot targets at close range and from far away. They learn to shoot while standing, lying on the ground, or moving.

Every few months, SWAT operators are tested on their marksmanship. They are expected to be expert shots at all times. A common test is to shoot rifles at small targets 100 yards (91 m) away. They must hit between 85 to 90 percent of their targets or lose their spot on the SWAT team.

A SWAT team practices breaking into a building to capture criminals.

## Simulation training

Shooting and hitting paper targets is an important ability. However, real-life crime scenes are much more complex. Several times per month, SWAT operators sharpen their skills by practicing in full gear against simulated criminals. Some of these foes even shoot back.

Simulation training is held at abandoned houses or other properties such as office buildings or airports. Wooden mazes can also be built near police shooting ranges. Moving targets and mannequins add to the realism.

Sometimes simulation training involves using other SWAT team members who pose as criminals. Each side uses simulated ammunition called Simunition. It is similar to paintballs and leaves a paint splat. This training ammo is used in real guns that have been modified to fire the special rounds. Getting hit by Simunition ammo hurts. It can leave bruises and welts, which makes the training more realistic.

Simulation training covers many kinds of crime scenarios. SWAT operators can realistically practice arresting criminals inside barricaded buildings. They can also learn how to rescue hostages. As they train, SWAT operators learn from their mistakes. They repeat scenarios over and over until they work flawlessly as a team.

Simunition (left, in blue) next to a real bullet. Simunition comes in several colors. The ammo is similar to paintballs and leaves a paint splat where it strikes.

## Special skills

In addition to marksmanship and simulation training, SWAT operators practice many other skills. Law enforcement techniques are improved through constant training.

Many cities, such as Miami, Florida, are near oceans or large lakes. SWAT departments in these places train for situations around water. Possible water operations might include hostage rescues on boats, or the use of SCUBA gear at night to swim to a remote beach and surprise criminals.

Many urban areas have high-rise apartments and office buildings. In some barricaded crime scenes, entering from the ground level is too dangerous. SWAT teams train to enter buildings from the rooftops. They can rappel down using ropes from a level above the criminals.

In some cases, helicopters can either land on rooftops, or SWAT operators can fast-rope down thick, 40-foot (12-m) -long ropes. They grip it with their hands and feet in order to control their descent. Once on the roof, they can enter the building and then quickly go down stairways to the crime scene.

SWAT team members practice rappelling down a building to free a hostage.

# SWAT EQUIPMENT

**SWAT officers are never sure what kinds of weapons** criminals might use, so they have to be ready for anything. SWAT operators carry advanced equipment and firearms that are not normally used by regular police officers.

SWAT officers are equipped with all the tools and firearms they may need for dangerous crime scenes.

## Uniforms and duty belts

In the past, most SWAT officers wore military-like uniforms and combat boots. Many departments still use them. The olive green camouflage patterns set elite SWAT operators apart from other police officers. In recent years, more and more police departments started issuing new SWAT uniforms. They come in traditional police colors, such as black or navy blue. The new uniforms are designed to be less intimidating to the public.

Most SWAT operators wear a combat belt (sometimes called a battle belt). It is a heavy-duty version of a regular patrol officer's duty belt. It can carry a holster, a med-pac pouch, flashlight, a knife, ammunition, or extra handcuffs or Flex-Cuffs.

## Body armor

SWAT teams need extra protection because of their hazardous jobs. Operators wear Level IV tactical vests. These are heavy-duty versions of police body armor. They are designed with dense fiber, such as Kevlar, that resists bullet penetration. Tactical vests also have ceramic armor plates in the chest and back area. The plates give extra protection against high-powered rifle bullets. Some vests are modular, with detachable shoulder and neck protection.

In recent years, tactical vests have become much lighter and more comfortable to wear over long periods of time. Even so, vests with equipment attached can weigh up to 30 pounds (14 kg). Older vests with steel plates can weigh up to 65 pounds (29 kg).

Vests are not perfect. Bullets sometimes penetrate them, or strike an unprotected part of the body. Some operators write their blood type on their vests. If they are shot and become unconscious, emergency room doctors can then know which type of blood to give them if necessary.

In addition to tactical vests, SWAT operators wear protective helmets and eyewear. Ballistic helmets are made of layers of Kevlar and resin. They are designed to stop or deflect bullets. They weigh about three pounds (1.4 kg).

**Flash Bang Grenade**

## Flash bang grenades

Flash bang grenades are also called stun grenades. SWAT operators simply call them "bangs." They create a deafening noise, a blinding flash, and smoke. This disorients suspects, giving SWAT officers the element of surprise and precious moments to enter a building. To deploy a flash bang, a pin is pulled. It is then quickly tossed through an open door or window.

## Firearms

Many SWAT team operators can choose their personal sidearm. A popular choice is the SIG Sauer P226 semiautomatic 9mm pistol. US Navy SEALs use the same handgun.

**SIG Sauer P226**

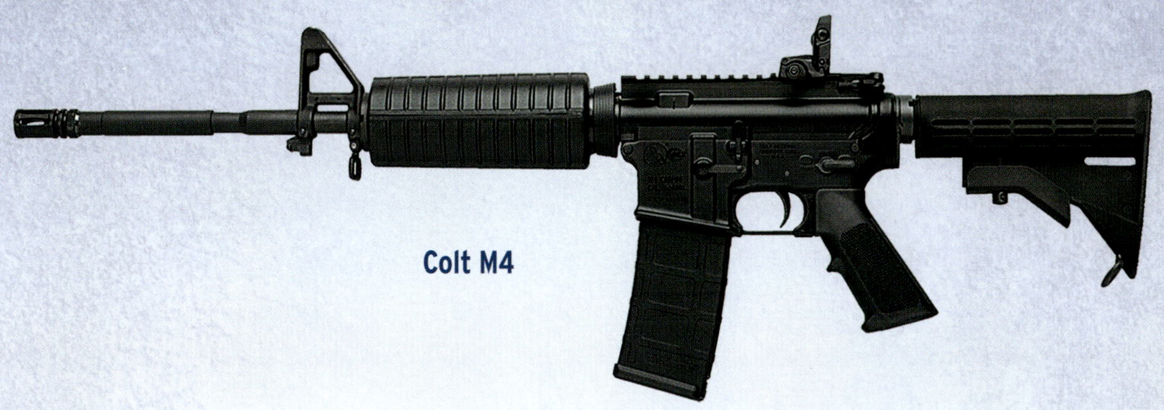

**Colt M4**

Other sidearms used by SWAT operators include the powerful Colt .45, and 9mm and .40-caliber models by Glock, Beretta, and Heckler & Koch. Most operators wear their handguns in a holster strapped to the side of their leg. This allows for a faster draw.

The most common rifles used by SWAT are carbines. They are lighter and have a shorter barrel than regular rifles. They are effective in cramped spaces, such as the inside of a house. The Colt M4 carbine is similar to the US military's M16 assault rifle. It can be fitted with night gunsights.

For close fighting where increased firepower is needed, submachine guns and shotguns are extremely effective. The Heckler & Koch MP5 9mm automatic submachine gun is common with law enforcement agencies around the world, including SWAT teams. There are many kinds of shotguns used by SWAT operators, including those made by Mossberg, Remington, and Benelli. Shotguns have extreme stopping power. They can also be used to blow open door locks.

## Tear gas

Tear gas, also called CS gas, causes eye pain and temporary blindness. It also irritates the nose and lungs, causing uncontrollable coughing. It is used during riots to force large crowds to scatter. It is also used to flush out criminals who have barricaded themselves inside buildings. Tear gas comes in canisters that are tossed by hand or shot by a launcher.

To protect themselves, SWAT operators wear M50 or similar gas masks. They form a tight seal against the face. As contaminated air is inhaled, it is purified by carbon filters.

## Multi-shot launchers

Multi-shot launchers are also called riot guns. They can be used against violent suspects at a safe distance. Most can fire six shots before reloading. They can deploy tear gas and shoot less-lethal sponge rounds. Sponge rounds stun suspects. They look like large bullets, but with plastic bodies and foam nose cones. When fired, the blue tip separates and strikes suspects hard enough to cause pain and confusion. This allows SWAT operators to rush in and detain them.

**Multi-Shot Launcher and Ammo**

Tracked tactical robots can perform tasks that are too dangerous for SWAT officers.

## Robots and drones

Tactical robots and drones are new tools used by SWAT teams. All are controlled by an officer from a safe distance away. Flying drones can give a bird's-eye view of a barricaded suspect's location. Heavy-duty tracked robots have been used to defuse bombs, scout crime scenes, and even disarm suspects. The Recon Scout Throwbot is a two-wheeled robot the size of a toy car. It can be tossed into a building and then send real-time video with its built-in camera.

# Chapter 7

# SWAT VEHICLES

The most common vehicles used by SWAT teams are armored cars. They transport SWAT operators to a crime scene and protect them against gunfire. They are commonly called armored tactical vehicles, or armored rescue vehicles. They are modified versions of armored vehicles used by the military.

BearCats are wheeled vehicles that can hold about 12 people, including a driver.

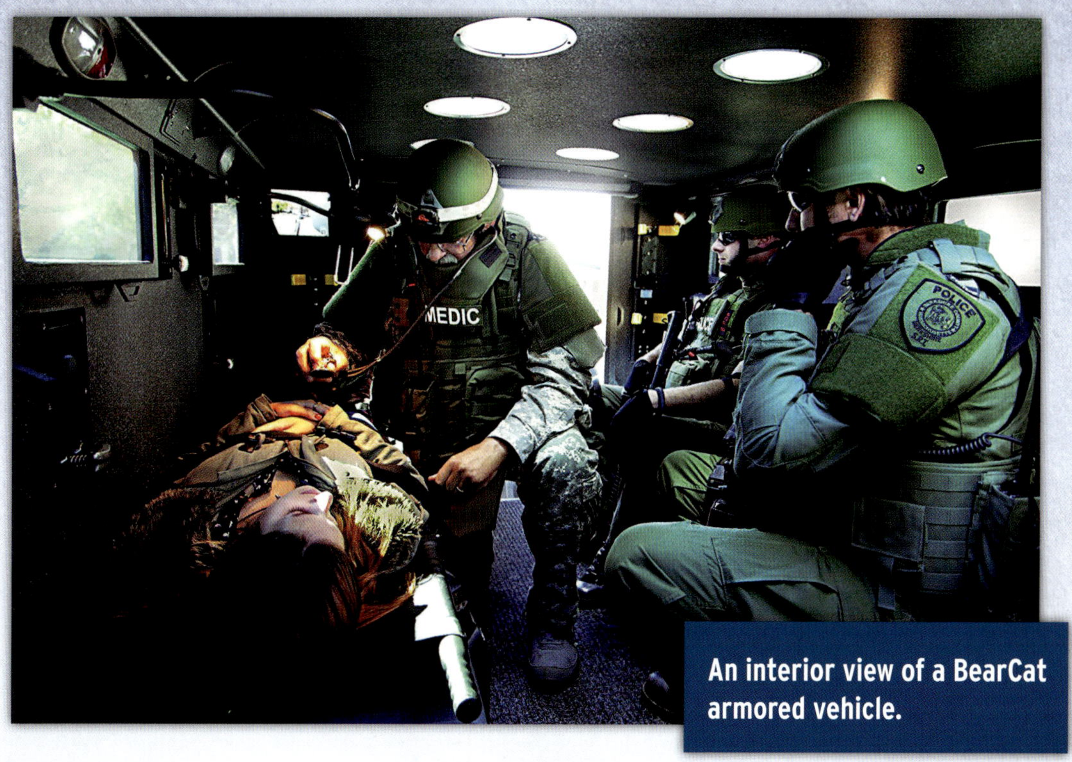

An interior view of a BearCat armored vehicle.

Many SWAT departments use BearCats. They are made by Lenco Industries. They have thick, steel armor and bullet-proof windows that can stop most gunfire from penetrating, even bullets fired from high-powered rifles. The floor is resistant to bombs, and an operator can stand up through a roof hatch to shoot. A battering ram can be fitted to the front of a BearCat to punch open barricaded doors.

A BearCat has aluminum running boards along both sides and the rear. Just before they arrive at the scene, SWAT operators can stand on the running boards. That allows them to jump off quickly at the crime scene all at once, instead of bailing one-by-one out the back door.

## Mobile command centers

A mobile command center is a large, motor home-like vehicle. Filled with electronic equipment and communications gear, it is parked a short distance from the crime scene. From this staging area, SWAT commanders and negotiators work safely from the command post, communicating by radio with operators at the scene.

Mobile command centers have state-of-the-art communications equipment. They are connected to SWAT operators and other law enforcement agencies by satellite radio, cellular, and landline telephones. They can receive live video feeds from the crime scene, and also monitor important weather and news reports.

Mobile command centers connect negotiators and field commanders with operators at the crime scene.

## Helicopters

The most common job of a SWAT helicopter is to scout locations before a raid. When SWAT operators are at a crime scene, helicopters can fly overhead and report the location of suspects who are hiding or have fled. Helicopters are also sometimes used to transport operators to locations that are difficult to reach, such as the rooftops of tall buildings.

# Chapter 8

# TEAM SPECIALISTS

**S**WAT **operators can handle many kinds of weapons and** tactics. There are some specialist jobs, however, that require additional training. They include tactical emergency medics, hand-to-hand combat specialists, weapons systems, explosives, and investigators. Two of the most common specialists include crisis negotiators and snipers.

## Crisis negotiators

The goal of a skilled SWAT negotiator is to talk to suspects, get their trust, and convince them to surrender. Most SWAT standoffs end without a single shot being fired.

When a standoff begins, negotiators make contact with the suspects, either through a bullhorn or with a telephone in a mobile command center. Sometimes, suspects calm down right away and surrender after talking with a SWAT negotiator. However, talks can last for hours. Only when violence seems imminent is the order given for the rest of the SWAT team to move in.

## Snipers

SWAT snipers provide "overwatch" protection to the rest of the team. If necessary, they can shoot violent suspects at a safe distance with high-powered rifles. More often, snipers relay information about suspects that they observe through their rifle scopes. The other operators depend on snipers to give them real-time information about what suspects are doing.

A SWAT sniper watches from a rooftop overlooking a crime scene.

# Chapter 9

# ENTRY TACTICS

**T**he riskiest part of an operator's job is entering a building with suspects inside. Entry teams never know how much danger is on the other side of a barricaded door. To minimize the danger, SWAT tactics are designed to confuse and frighten suspects. By "going big and bold," with as much noise and display of force as possible, operators try to make criminals so scared that they give up without a fight. A perfect operation is when not a single shot is fired, and everyone including the suspects are safe.

Breachers are the first operators to take action. After stunning suspects with a flash bang grenade tossed through a window, they spring into action. The simplest way to break down a door is with a battering ram. They are made of iron and weigh about 40 pounds (18 kg). When smashed into locks or door handles, they break through wood and pop open doors. Regular sledge hammers and metal pry bars are also effective. Explosives are rarely used, but work well against heavily reinforced steel doors.

Battering rams are nicknamed "slammers."

## Breaching fortified doors

Suspects in drug houses sometimes fortify their doors with exterior cages. SWAT operators use metal harpoons or hooks to quickly attach fabric straps to the cages, doors, or even windows. The team's armored vehicle then pulls the straps, ripping the obstacles off the house.

## Arrest teams

As soon as an opening is breached, an arrest team rushes in, single file. This is called "stacking up." The first operator in the stack might use an entry shield, also called a ballistic shield, to deflect bullets.

As they enter, the operators loudly announce themselves, "Police department! Search warrant!" Going through an entry point is like entering a funnel. Cops call them "fatal funnels." The first operator through is the one "on point." This officer is the first one suspects see, and might shoot at. If any of the operators stop in the entry, everything gets clogged up behind them. It is important to keep moving.

The SWAT operators enter the building with guns drawn. They fan out and face in different directions to make sure there are no hidden dangers. Then they move deeper inside the building, clearing rooms and making arrests.

After the entry team has completely cleared a building, a search team and police detectives look for things like illegal drugs and firearms. If the operation has been perfectly successful, everyone is safe, including the community. Sometimes violence occurs, but that is part of the job. Though there is danger, SWAT operators take satisfaction in helping make their communities safer places to live.

# GLOSSARY

**arrest** – When a person suspected of committing a crime is taken into custody by a law enforcement officer.

**barricade situation** – When a person maintains a position of cover or concealment and ignores or resists law enforcement personnel. The person is usually armed with a weapon.

**blood type** – Every human has one of four blood types: A, B, AB, or O. The type, which is inherited from a person's parents, depends on the substances found or missing from red blood cells.

**detain** – When a police officer stops a person for brief questioning, possibly before a formal arrest.

**Flex-Cuffs** – Plastic zip ties used instead of handcuffs. Unlike heavier metal cuffs, they don't need a key or to be sanitized and returned to the arresting officer. They are cut off and thrown away once a suspect is transported to the police station or jail. SWAT teams often use Flex-Cuffs when working at riots or protests, where large numbers of people might be detained or arrested.

**less lethal** – A device, object, or weapon that would not kill a living thing. Also called less-than-lethal.

**med-pac pouch** – A first aid pouch that attaches to a SWAT team member's  combat belt. Inside would be emergency medical gear such as bandages, gauze, and tourniquets.

**semiautomatic** – A firearm that shoots once with every pull of the trigger. It automatically reloads, ready for the next shot.

**staging area** – A location where operators check in for duty.

**warrant** – An arrest warrant authorizes the police to arrest someone suspected of committing a crime. A search warrant allows the search of a person, vehicle, or building.

## ONLINE RESOURCES

To learn more about SWAT, visit abdobooklinks.com or scan this QR code. These links are routinely monitored and updated to provide the most current information available.

# INDEX